Beowulf
and the
Monster

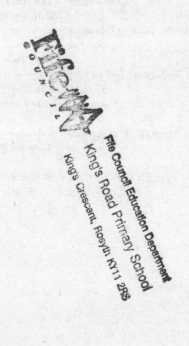

Other brilliant stories to collect:

Aesop's Fables
Malorie Blackman

Puss in Boots
Diana Wynne Jones

Hansel and Gretel
Henrietta Branford

The Seal Hunter
Tony Mitton

The Goose Girl
Gillian Cross

Cockadoodle-doo,
Mr Sultana!
Michael Morpurgo

The Snow Queen
Berlie Doherty

The Pied Piper
K.M. Peyton

The Twelve Dancing Princesses
Anne Fine

Mossycoat
Philip Pullman

Grey Wolf, Prince Jack and the
Firebird
Alan Garner

The Simple Giant
Alan Temperley

The Three Heads in the Well
Susan Gates

Rapunzel
Jacqueline Wilson

The Six Swan Brothers
Adèle Geras

Rumpelstiltskin
Kit Wright

Beowulf and the Monster

Retold by
Brian Patten

Illustrated by
Chris Riddell

■SCHOLASTIC
Home of the Story

For Edward Stoddart,
a Beowulf in the making.

Scholastic Children's Books,
Commonwealth House, 1–19 New Oxford Street,
London WC1A 1NU, UK
a division of Scholastic Ltd
London ~ New York ~ Toronto ~ Sydney ~ Auckland
Mexico City ~ New Delhi ~ Hong Kong

First published by Scholastic Ltd, 1999

Text copyright © Brian Patten, 1999
Illustrations copyright © Chris Riddell, 1999

ISBN 0 590 19685 5

Printed by Cox and Wyman Ltd, Reading, Berks.

2 4 6 8 10 9 7 5 3

The right of Brian Patten and Chris Riddell to be identified as the
author and illustrator respectively of this work has been asserted by
them in accordance with the Copyright, Designs and Patents Act, 1988.

Centuries ago, when the land was covered in forests and wolves and demons crouched in every shadow, there lived a powerful warrior king. He was as famous for his generosity as for his strength, and when his last great battle was over and peace declared, he decided to hold a

wonderful party to celebrate.

He sent out invitations to the rich and poor alike, and then set about building a gigantic hall in which to hold his special feast. All his people came to help him build the hall, from the oldest to the youngest, and the new building rose quickly in a vast clearing in the forest.

It was a majestic hall, with wooden towers and pinnacles that reached higher than the highest trees. It was the tallest, finest building that had ever been seen in the land. And the king was proud of it. Nothing as grand had existed in his kingdom before. It became known as the Great Hall.

As soon as the Hall was finished the party began. It was to be the feast to end all feasts. It began one morning as the sun rose and then continued day after day, night after night. Long tables sagged under the

weight of the food, and the revellers sagged under the effect of the drink. It made their heads spin and caused them to sing louder and louder and to dance more and more wildly.

All this happened in distant times, when wild boars roamed the countryside, and moon-mad wolves slunk through the night. It was a time when the world was heaped with mysteries.

The feast was a roaring success. The music and singing grew louder and louder, and the louder it became the

farther the sound travelled, until it was heard beyond the forest by the one being whom no one in their wildest dreams would have invited to the feast.

It was heard by the monster, Grendel.

Grendel lived in the fens and the foul-smelling marshland beyond the forest. The marsh was littered with oozing pools and the festering remains of dead otters and decaying fish. No one, not even the bravest warrior, went there. The place reeked of evil.

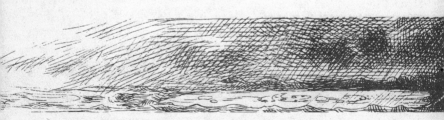

Evil suited Grendel. Half-man, half-fiend, he was an extraordinary creature with supernatural strength. Covered in a green, horny skin that no sword could cut through, he came from a race of sea monsters, giants, goblins, and other outcasts from the human race.

Grendel was in the habit of sleeping for centuries, and he had been

asleep so long that the king and his subjects had forgotten his existence. If they thought of him at all, they remembered him as a creature from legends. That was their big mistake.

And now the sound of music and human laughter had awakened him. He rose from his nest of rats' bones and sat listening among the slithering eels and the scent of decay.

He hated the music. He hated it because he hated the humans that made it. He hated it with a hatred that burnt bright as a star. He hated it as only a demon can hate. It reminded

him of what an outcast he was. In his ears that music sounded like the buzzing of flies.

While the king and his warriors feasted and drank, the monster Grendel shrugged off a century of sleep.

Why should people be happy? he wondered. Why should they make music and sing and hold great feasts while he sat alone in a stinking bog?

He was full of jealousy and hatred.

I'll destroy their merriment, he thought.

Grendel slouched through the marshland and forest towards the Great Hall. As he passed, the creatures of the night quaked with fear and fell silent. The owls stopped hooting. Frogs stopped croaking. The nightjar's song stuck in its throat. Badgers returned to their underground sets. Even the shadows themselves recoiled from Grendel's presence as he flowed through the night like poison spilt from a cup.

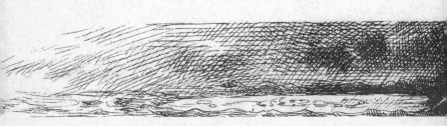

Grendel waited hidden among the trees until the Great Hall had fallen silent and the last revellers had wandered to their homes, sleepy and exhausted by the feasting.

The king had left his favourite warriors to guard the Hall, but because there was peace in the land they did not take their guard-duty seriously. They fell asleep, and did

not hear Grendel croaking his terrible
song as he moved out from the
shadows towards them:

"Sweet human meat's the best to eat,
And human bones the best to grind.
Human blood will flow again
And cold terror haunt the human mind."

A century of sleep had whetted
Grendel's appetite. He crashed into
the Great Hall and surprised the
sleeping warriors. He plucked off
their limbs as if they were petals.
Blood filled the Great Hall. It dripped

from the rafters and flowed out into the moonlight. Grendel ate his fill, then gathering into his powerful arms the warriors he could not eat, the demon slouched back off to his dwelling-place in the fetid marshland pools.

Now let them sing, he thought.

The next morning people were struck dumb with terror when they saw what

had happened in the Great Hall. It did not take long for them to realize it could have only been Grendel who had committed the dreadful crime. No human could have done what the monster had done, and their suspicions were confirmed when they saw the trail of blood that led out to the marshland.

The king was in despair. His greatest and most trusted warriors had all been slaughtered, and he himself had grown too old to wage war against such a creature as Grendel. He sat down on the earth

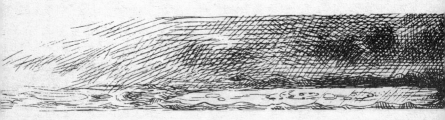

and cried and sang an ancient
lament:

"I grow old and my bones grow cold,
The fire of my youth has gone.
My strength is like the receding tide
And hopes have I none."

And his subjects wept with him.

After a century without the taste of
human blood, that taste was as fresh
and sweet as blackberries to Grendel.
He came back again and again. Night
after night he returned to the village,

searching the surrounding houses for unwary humans. And each night he sat brooding in the Great Hall like a bloated spider inside its web.

Soon no one dared sleep in their homes. People would only visit the village in the daylight, when they were sure Grendel would not come. And as for the Great Hall, they shunned it both day and night.

The Great Hall, their pride and joy, stood empty. Darkness fell upon it. Owls colonized its rafters and rats scurried about its floor.

It was the greatest disaster that had ever befallen the king and his people. At night they all hid in the forest like wild animals and whenever Grendel found a careless sleeper, he would drag them to the Great Hall and devour them.

There was no laughter in the kingdom. No songs. No feasting. No joy. Stories of the monster's terrible deeds spread far and wide. Warriors came from distant lands, all hoping to prove themselves heroes and destroy Grendel, but none was quite great enough.

The first warrior to come had a magic bow.

"I'm the greatest warrior of all," he said. "I will destroy Grendel with my bow."

The king hoped against hope that the stranger could fulfil his boast. At

dusk when Grendel rose up from his nest of rats' bones and came to the village, the warrior took out a magic arrow and aimed it at Grendel's heart. But the arrow might as well have been a feather for all the harm it did.

The next warrior to come had a magic dagger. It might as well have been a reed for all the harm it did.

Other warriors came, and many lost their lives. Some were boastful fools and others were brave. All the same, none could defeat Grendel, who merely taunted them with his terrible song:

"Sweet human meat's the best to eat,
And human bones the best to grind.
Human blood will flow again
And cold terror haunt the human mind."

And so the years passed and the dust lay thick as snow in the Great Hall. People's spirits were broken, and no one took pride in themselves or their land. Crops failed in the fields. Houses fell to rack and ruin. Paths became overgrown and were forgotten. Warriors had long ceased to come and pit their strength against Grendel. More human bones than rats' bones

littered his nest now.

Then early one frosty morning as winter took hold of the kingdom, a boat was seen sailing over the horizon. It was unlike any other boat that had sailed on the sea before it. Its prow was carved with the face of a dragon and its mast looked like the antlers of a stag. The deck glittered with flecks of frost that the rising sun transformed into rubies.

It was such a wonderful sight the old king was informed immediately. He stood on the cliff top supported by two of his servants and watched as the

vessel pulled into a rocky bay.

A young man stepped from the boat and strode with ease up the cliff's steep path.

The moment the old king stared into the youth's clear eyes he knew who had come to his land. For years rumours had reached him about a remarkable youth who lived across the Northern Rim of the world, a boy with the strength of thirty men, who was nevertheless gentle and hard to provoke to anger.

"Are you Beowulf?" he asked.

"Yes," said Beowulf. "And I have

come to face Grendel. I would have come some time ago, if it were not that the time to face him is written in the stars."

"And do the stars say the time is now?" asked the king.

"Yes," said Beowulf. "Tonight we will light candles in the Great Hall and I will wait for him there."

So many warriors had come before Beowulf and been slain and their bones used to line Grendel's nest that the old king felt afraid for Beowulf. But his fear for the young man's life was not as strong as his desire to rid his kingdom

of the demon who haunted it.

He welcomed Beowulf gladly, and together they set off for the Great Hall.

When they arrived the sun had begun to set and the villagers were leaving for their hidey-holes in the forest. The king helped Beowulf light the Great Hall with candles, which Beowulf said would confuse

Grendel. Then, greatly troubled in his mind, he too departed. Beowulf was left to face the perils of the coming night alone.

The young warrior stood at the entrance to the Hall and looked out at the deserted village. Nothing stirred. A deathly silence hung over the place as the light retreated. Shadows crept over the now abandoned houses.

They crept through the forest and across the marshland where, like severed fingers, they poked Grendel awake. The monster sniffed the coming night, and rising from his nest among the putrid pools, he crooned his vile song:

"Sweet human meat's the best to eat,
And human bones the best to grind.
Human blood will flow again
And cold terror haunt the human mind."

So singing, he set off for the Great Hall, his nose sniffing the air for the

scent of human blood.

Now Beowulf was the most powerful warrior on earth, stronger than any other mortal, and he was no fool. He had heard tell of Grendel's strength and cunning, and knew he had to match both with his own. He must unsettle Grendel. He understood that the best fighters kept their wits about them at all times, so he must make Grendel so furious and blind with rage that the monster would make a fatal error. He unbuckled his sword and put it aside, knowing from the many tales

he'd heard that swords were useless
on the monster's skin.

When shadow merged with shadow,
Grendel came. From the marshy
wilderness, through mists and swamp-
born fogs, the hideous monster made
his way to the Great Hall he hated so
bitterly. He came to its massive door
and tried to push it open as he had
done night after night, year after year.

But the door was locked and bolted. He was furious that the villagers could have done such a thing after so long. He hammered the iron-laced oak with his bare fists and smashed it inward, as if it were no more substantial than a wren's nest.

As Grendel entered, his monstrous shadow filled the Hall. His anger increased ten-fold when he saw that

humans had dared to enter before him and fill the place with candles. The Hall's great beams flickered in their light, and cobwebs hung down like grotesque decorations. Between the groups of candles were great pools of darkness.

Why had they done this? For what possible reason? For a moment the fiend's mind clouded over, and he stood rock-still and puzzled.

This gave time for Beowulf to study his foe. Hidden among the shadows, he picked a tiny pebble from the floor and tossed it in

Grendel's direction. Grendel turned, his ears alert to the faintest sound.

"What's that?" he bellowed.

"Merely a mouse," whispered Beowulf.

"What mouse is it that smells of human blood and talks with a human tongue?"

"The mouse that will devour you," whispered Beowulf.

Silently, Beowulf climbed up on to the rafters above the Hall, and while Grendel stomped about below, he tossed another pebble.

"What's that?" roared Grendel.

"Merely an owl," whispered Beowulf.

"What owl is it that smells of human blood and talks with a human tongue?"

"The owl that will devour you," said Beowulf.

He dropped from the rafters like an avenging angel.

The monster was so befuddled with talk of owls and mice, and so full of anger at being taunted, that when Beowulf dropped down beside him he was caught unawares. Beowulf gripped the creature's arm and

Grendel cried out in surprise. The feel of Beowulf's grip and its strength were alien to him. Nothing on earth or in the supernatural world had threatened his existence before. The monster had reigned supreme for centuries.

Now Grendel spun round, flinging out his arm and throwing Beowulf off balance. But in a moment Beowulf was back, his powerful fist smashing Grendel's jaw, and scattering his teeth like black pearls.

As they rolled on the floor of the Great Hall, first one then the other

had the upper hand. Grendel clawed at Beowulf's face till Beowulf was blinded by his own blood. But still he clung to the demon, crushing its neck with the power of thirty men. In the fury of the fight the Hall was wrecked. The banqueting table was smashed to smithereens and splinters stuck in the combatants' flesh. Human and monster blood was sprayed across the scarred walls, and still neither man nor monster gave ground.

Then the moment of victory came.

There was a sound like the cracking

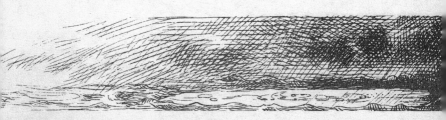

of a branch and the bone in Grendel's right arm snapped. For the first and only time he tasted defeat. Bellowing with despair Grendel looked through blood-dimmed eyes for the door, craving escape. But Beowulf held his good arm in a grip no man on earth could equal or endure, and the monster howled in anguish as he struggled to free himself.

Suddenly, with a final cry, Grendel managed to wrench himself free. He staggered out of the Hall, leaving behind him a river of blood. In his fury to escape, his arm and shoulder

had been torn off, and left in Beowulf's iron-like grip. Beowulf looked at it in amazed horror and flung it aside.

Back across the marshy wilderness the defeated monster stumbled, through the same mists and swamp-born fogs he had come from with such confidence. Soon he was home, and as the last flickerings of life faded from him,

he sank down through the lake that edged the foul-smelling marshland. Down he sank, deeper and deeper into the putrid depths, dying as he reached the very place of his birth.

And in that place, unknown to any human being, an even greater monster waited.

The next morning the sun rose over a different world. It glittered on beads

of water formed by the retreating frost, and the Hall's great roof shone as if it were wrapped in silver. The old king wept with happiness when he discovered the outcome of the fight. He hugged Beowulf like a son and ordered the Great Hall to be cleaned out and repaired. Grendel's severed arm was found and nailed above the entrance, so everyone could see for themselves how remarkable Beowulf's victory had been.

As the news spread, so Beowulf's fame spread. He was showered with gift after gift in gratitude: a gold-handled

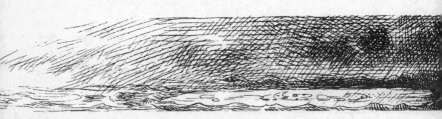

sword, a helmet embedded with jewels, seven of the finest stallions in the land.

The villagers abandoned their hidey-holes in the forest. Once more there was food and music. Once more people drank themselves dizzy. Once more they exhausted themselves dancing. Then after the celebrations they retired to their homes for the first time in years. Beowulf was given

the best room in the king's house where, exhausted by his victory, he fell into a deep sleep.

But then once again something stirred out in the fens and marsh-lands. Once again evil was abroad. Pools bubbled with poison, and Grendel's mother, the Hag, the first and most terrible witch in the world, rose to seek her revenge on those who had slain her son.

The Hagwitch, Grendel's mother, came that night, loping along the marshland paths like a monstrous

wolf. She was bent double with the weight of centuries, yet still almost twice the size of a human being. She swept through the village, blind with grief and rage.

"Who killed my son?" she howled. "What mortal killed him?"

But such was her fury that before anyone could speak, she had dragged them from their beds and, sinking her teeth into their necks, silenced them for ever. And then she was gone again, leaving behind a trail of death and destruction.

When those who had escaped the

Hagwitch's onslaught described her to the dismayed king, he remembered the legend of how Grendel's mother lived deep below the marshland lake, and realized it was she who had caused such mayhem.

The king summoned Beowulf and begged him to try and destroy her, as he had destroyed her son.

The king explained that according to legends the entrance to the Hagwitch's lair was protected by three chambers, each of which was blocked by three gigantic stones, so heavy no mortal could lift them.

"Then we are lost," said Beowulf. "She is well protected."

"Perhaps not," said the king. "There is some mystery surrounding the stones. It is said a clever man can make them move aside of their own accord."

"How can stones move of their own accord?" asked Beowulf.

The king simply shrugged. "How do youths kill monsters? There are many mysteries in the world, Beowulf. You must try for all our sakes," he said.

And so leaving the king and his people to care for the wounded, Beowulf set off alone to find Grendel's mother. She had left the village so covered in blood, her retreat was easy to follow. Her blood-splattered trail led him along the marshland paths. It led through groves of deformed trees and broken stumps grey with lichens. Rats scurried along the path ahead of

him. Crows blinked their tiny red eyes and hopped through the tangled branches like spies.

Although it was still daylight, the closer Beowulf came to the Hagwitch's lair, the colder the day seemed. He sensed she knew of his approach, and that she listened, her ears finely attuned to all manner of things that walked the surface of the earth.

The path snaked deep into the treacherous marshes. It passed fetid pools and crossed over weed-choked streams in which toads croaked and sang like a witch's choir. Beowulf came to the edge of a dark lake, over which hung a yellow mist that shut out the sun. The whole atmosphere of the place felt lifeless. The air itself seemed stale and jaundiced, trapped under a canopy of gloomy clouds.

Near the centre of the lake he saw Grendel's nest, deserted now.

Young Beowulf's heart drummed fast as he prepared to face the Hagwitch.

He clipped on his vest of chainmail. From its sheath he took a sword hardened by the blood of battles. He polished his dagger with poisonous herbs. Breathing slowly and deeply, he waded into the lake.

Sword in hand, he sank down through the murky depths. Eels wrapped themselves round his ankles. Leeches clung to his cheeks. He ignored them, sinking deeper and deeper until he came to a thin crust of rock on the lake's bottom. He plunged his sword into it as easily as a child might plunge its finger into a pie crust.

The river-bed opened, and he fell through it into the underground chambers that led to the Hagwitch's lair.

It was here he came upon the body of Grendel.

It had been laid out lovingly on a stone slab, and Beowulf felt a twinge of confusion as he looked upon that wretched face. To the Hagwitch no doubt it was a lovely face, the face of her only son. But Beowulf could not afford to feel sorry for her. What other monsters would she spawn to send scurrying to the face of the earth

if he felt compassion for her? No, it was his purpose to slay her.

Beowulf found the first of the three huge stones that blocked the way to the Hagwitch's lair. It was so huge he did not even attempt to move it. Instead he studied the stone, remembering what the old king had told him. "How can a clever man make a stone move of its own accord?" he wondered out loud.

As soon as he spoke, a transformation overtook the stone. Whereas once its centre had been smooth, now two thin lines appeared. They

widened, and as Beowulf stared in amazement, a pair of lips grew upon the surface of the stone.

"I am the first of the Riddle Stones," it said. "Answer my riddle and I will move aside." There was a moment's silence, and then the stone spoke again:

"Dressed in red,
I rob wisdom from the wisest man.
I cause the coward to be brave,
And lead the stupid to their grave."

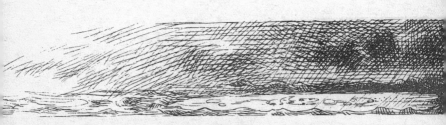

Beowulf thought the riddle easy.

"Wine is the answer," said Beowulf. "Drunk, even the wisest men are fools." He was right, and the stone moved aside. Behind it was a second chamber. Here an even greater Riddle Stone stood in his path, and the same thing happened. Lips grew out of the stone, and it spoke to him:

"I am the second of the Riddle Stones," it said. "Answer my riddle and I too will move aside.

"On the ground I move silently,
A proud and haughty thing,
But above the earth and water
My soft white garments sing."

Beowulf found this riddle harder than
the first, but again he answered
correctly. "The answer is Swan," he
said, "for though it is mute, when
the swan flies through the air its
wings make a sound like singing."
The second of the Riddle Stones
moved aside. In the third and final
chamber he found the most massive
stone of all.

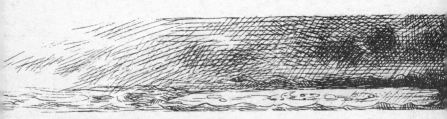

Although Beowulf did not know it, in the world above him night had fallen, and the darker it grew the more powerful grew the Hagwitch's strength. She was moving about now, vast and wolf-like beyond the final stone.

It, too, spoke to Beowulf:

"I am the third Riddle Stone.
Answer my riddle and you will find
The Hagwitch who haunts the
  human mind."

Beowulf listened intently as the lips in the stone wriggled in a gross parody of a human mouth:

"No doctor tries to heal my wounds.
In war no warrior befriends me.
Though enemies have I none,
I am scarred by battles gone."

Because he was a warrior, Beowulf found this riddle the simplest of all. "In war no warrior befriends a shield," he said, "so Shield is the answer."

Again he was right, and the final stone rolled aside.

Beyond the stone, Grendel's mother sat crouched in a nest of bones. From her eyes shone a green light that illuminated the chamber's walls and caused Beowulf's shadow to dance upon them like a doll.

Like Grendel, she too was covered in scales. The small, stiff hairs on her back crawled with lice. She swayed to and fro, now mewing like a cat, now growling like a wolf, and never for a moment taking her eyes from Beowulf's face.

She leapt towards him, and as she did so, Beowulf swung his massive sword. The end came more swiftly

than he could have ever imagined.

The sword struck the side of her neck with crushing force and shattered like glass. He flung the broken weapon aside. As she leapt upon him again, he grabbed a human bone from her nest and plunged it into her throat with almost super-human force. A fountain of green blood burst from her mouth and the Hagwitch fell back, dead.

Only when her body had turned cold did Beowulf approach it. He had overcome her so swiftly, he hardly dared believe his good fortune. He waited until even the lice had deserted the immobile body, then he dragged the bodies of the Hagwitch and her son to the lake's surface, and swam with them to the shore.

The bodies were laid out in the Great Hall, plain for all to see. This time, no one could doubt that the kingdom had been made safe by Beowulf.

Once again the old king wept with happiness. Once again fabulous gifts were showered upon Beowulf. Once again a great banquet was held in his honour. Once again many stories were told of his victory over the monsters.

This is but one of them.

Other stories to collect:

Aesop's Fables

Malorie Blackman
Illustrated by Patrice Aggs

Once upon a time there was a man named Aesop
who told stories full of wisdom…

Hansel and Gretel

Henrietta Branford
Illustrated by Lesley Harker

Once upon a time there were a brother and sister
who were left alone in the forest…

The Snow Queen

Berlie Doherty

Illustrated by Siân Bailey

Once upon a time there was a little boy whose
heart was turned to ice...

The Twelve
Dancing Princesses

Anne Fine

Illustrated by Debi Gliori

Once upon a time there were twelve princesses,
and no one knew why their shoes were full
of holes...

Grey Wolf, Prince Jack and the Firebird

Alan Garner

Illustrated by James Mayhew

Once upon a time there was a prince who set out
to seek the mysterious firebird…

Mossycoat

Philip Pullman

Illustrated by Peter Bailey

Once upon a time there was a beautiful girl whose
mother made her a magical, mossy coat…